SHAKEDOWN

J. Gunnar Grey

δ

Dingbat Publishing

SHAKEDOWN
Copyright © 2012 by J. Gunnar Grey
ISBN 978-1-940520-32-2

Published 2014 in the United States of America
Dingbat Publishing
Humble, Texas

Originally published 2012 by Astraea Press

Cover photo © 123rf.com and Magali Parise
Interior photo © 123rf.com and Aleksandr
Ugorenkov

For veterans of all varieties.

1

McKittrick Canyon
Guadalupe Mountains National Park
Culberson County, far West Texas

"Captain Kelly Bonham? Here he is." The SUV's driver punctuated his words full stop by slamming the vehicle's door. "Your retired war dog."

Yeah. Right. Bonnie rubbed her hands on her fatigue pants. Silly, to feel nervous over a dog. It wasn't like she'd accepted a blind date or anything outrageous. Dogs generally liked her and the more she saw of dogs, the more she preferred them to pretty much every unmarried man she knew. But still her palms itched, as if she'd done something stupid and expected to regret it.

She bent sideways and peered in at the SUV's back seat. Through the tinted side windows, all she could see was a dark outline, sitting stiffly upright. The outline seemed to be staring at her. *Sure, great. Make me even more nervous.*

The driver trudged around the SUV's front bumper, a Texas Rangers ball cap tugged down crookedly over his eyes. His lopsided grin tucked up his cheek on one side, leaving the other side of his face serious, and he set a clipboard and two stuffed file folders on the hood in passing.

"His name's Pojo," the driver said. "That's Papa Oscar Juliet Oscar. He's a registered German Shepherd, but not suitable for showing." He popped open the rear door and held it for her with a flourish.

Again Bonnie wiped her hands and leaned over.

From the shadows, the most incredible pair of eyes stared back at her. Not the usual canine brown or black — but amber, gleaming pools of expensive, honey-toned Baltic amber, the sort of thing usually seen strung into a rich woman's necklace. Wary, thoughtful eyes, staring without blinking as if weighing her in the balance. A shock rippled along Bonnie's spine. This wasn't a dog who'd wash her face, chase a ball, roll over for a tummy rub. This was a dog who made his own decisions. And he was making one right now.

Without looking away, he yawned, showing off an impressive collection of huge, glistening teeth, a dark mouth, an amazingly long tongue. His jaws stretched so wide, her head started to spin at the cavernous space opening before her. Then he snapped his jaws closed, teeth clacking.

And looked away as if she no longer existed.

Oh, hell. Had she ever made a mistake.

Something in her chest plummeted to her abdomen and she swallowed. But her dry throat refused to cooperate. "He's a bomb sniffer, right?" As opposed to something trained to chew her limbs off, one by one.

"An explosives detection dog, retired." The driver leaned in past her, hooked on a leash, and unsnapped the red nylon harness from the seatbelt. "Come on, Pojo."

For a moment the brute didn't move, actually leaned away from the leash's gentle tug. Maybe he thought it was all a mistake, too; maybe he'd refuse even to get out of the SUV, and a cowardly sort of relief washed through her. When the dog reluctantly turned and jumped from the back seat to the ground, lithe and graceful as a cat, Bonnie shivered. He didn't look back at her.

"He's what's called a blue Shepherd." The driver rambled on, as if nothing had happened. "See how his lips and nose are dark grey, instead of black? It's a genetic dilution and considered a fault. They're born with blue eyes, too, but those change as the puppies get older."

Pojo stalked away, head down, sniffing at the scrubby mountain grass. He turned and in the slanting evening sunlight, the washed-out hue of his mask and saddle became more obvious against his clear tan ruff and brindled hindquarters. Along his level back, several chunks of shorter fur rippled as he circled around them at the end of the leash.

Still ignoring her.

"So he was injured? Badly?"

"Not him, no. He and his handler were sniffing out a minefield near Khost, and the handler stumbled over a tripwire. One of them bounding anti-personnel mines." He rubbed the back of his neck and ducked his head. "Cut the handler in half, but Pojo only caught a few bits of stray shrapnel."

So the dog had seen his handler killed. At the thought, something inside Bonnie squirmed. That sounded like serious trauma and not a good thing at all. People went round the bend from less. One of her NATO team members had post-traumatic stress disorder and the first time he'd flashed back, he'd had screaming fits in the hospital, loud enough to be heard in the next hall over. He'd rolled out of bed, taking the bed with him; he'd had to be sat on and medicated.

One clear ray of golden sunlight splashed across Pojo, backlighting him and darkening that grey to charcoal, then he stepped past it, nose cutting through tufts of grass and snuffling loudly. What happened when a war dog flashed back? Considering those teeth, did she want to stick around and find out?

The driver held out the leash. She didn't want to take it; the brute on the leash's end twisted her about somewhere deep inside. But already the red nylon was winding around her legs. If she didn't take it, Pojo was going to tie them together and the driver was too much a Southern country boy for her taste. She slipped her hand through the loop and stepped away.

Time to shake her down, boys.

The twisting inside tightened at the thought. In the days of sail, a newly built ship, with a new crew and a new captain, would take a short, noncombatant cruise first thing off the stocks. The captain would feel out the ship's behavior, the officers would sort out the crew, and the crew would learn their duties. A shakedown cruise, it was called.

She was going to shake it down with a dog who had more teeth than the law allowed, a dog with a brain that might or might not be in fully functional condition. A dog that clearly wasn't impressed by her at all.

He still hadn't looked at her since jumping from the SUV.

The driver unloaded a giant bag of expensive dog food, carried it through her open cabin door, and reappeared without it. He scribbled a note on the clipboard's paper, scratched an X beside one line, and held it out. "Sign on the line, and he's yours."

Decision time.

That twisting rebelled and panic spiraled up into her throat, closing it off. She couldn't do this, didn't want to do this. She was an electronics technician, an intelligence officer — not a dog handler or canine psychologist. This beast needed a specialist, someone who could help him adjust to civilian life. Someone who'd know when the time was right to cut short the experiment and put him down.

As if he read her thought, Pojo lifted his head from the lawn and glared at her, some trick of the light making his amber eyes gleam from within. Like a dog possessed by something evil, something that wanted to rip her heart out and play chew-toy with it.

Or a dog who'd written her off at first sight.

She'd proven her worth during the war. To the team, to her commanding officer, to herself. No need to prove it to a possibly crazy dog.

Then again, it was entirely possible he wasn't. Not crazy, that is. And that would make her—

Bonnie pushed the leash up her wrist, grabbed the clipboard and pen, and signed.

The driver started shuffling papers. "I set his records on your kitchen counter. Here's a receipt—" he handed it over "—and congratulations on your newest family member."

Yeah. Right. So much for the family tree.

★ ★ ★ ★

"All right, kiddo. It's just you and me."

With the SUV and its rumbling engine gone, silence descended on Frijole Ridge. Around her, the clearing atop the mountain's shoulder seemed to expand — the SUV, the driver, the decision all had crowded her, and only with everything settled could she sense the surrounding stone and forest again. The sheer rock face reared above her log cabin, folding a cleft around its rear wall like an open book propped behind a little wooden box, and the forest of pine, oak, ash, and autumn-hued bigtooth maple flowed down the steep slope into the canyon below.

Beyond the canyon, the sun perched atop McKittrick Ridge, fat and golden, and thin streamers of orange and pink stretched along the horizon. The forest canopy below ruffled, cat's paws of wind stirring the branches tipped with reds and golds, and then the breeze rolled up the slope for the first time since morning. Bonnie closed her eyes as the canyon's warmth breathed across her face. Not much more of that left; the nights were already hinting it might be time to wake up the fireplace.

"Guess I need to show you our boundaries, kid. Whaddya say?"

Pojo had again stretched the leash as far as he could. He sat stiff and erect, hindlegs primly folded, his big rounded ears focused like twin radar antennas into the canyon, his nose twitching. The breeze combed through his ruff, little tufts of thick fur waving across the red nylon harness. His bottle-brush tail stretched out behind him, tip quivering. So many scents would be carried on that breeze — mule deer, javelina, coyotes, maybe even the cougar the park rangers had mentioned last time loneliness had driven her to the station. It was a whole new world for this war dog. Perhaps the interest it aroused in him would be the calming influence he needed.

Even if he wouldn't look at her.

"Pojo."

One ear flicked her way. He stood, shook out his coat, tugged against the leash, and then sat again, staring down into the canyon.

Nope, he wasn't going to make this easy. *Males. Why does everything have to be a fight?*

Bonnie sucked in a deep, slow breath. She could let him ignore her, but that was an invitation for him to walk all over her in the future. A better idea was — not to beat him up, but let him know who was boss. Who led the pack, as a canine psychologist might say.

She didn't look at him again. Sauce for the gander. "Pojo, come."

A soft sound, neither a whine nor a sigh but something indescribable in between, rose from the tense dog.

If this didn't work, he really would consider her useless. Or worse, ineffectual and helpless. With a dog this big, she couldn't afford that. She took another deep breath for luck, ignored her hammering pulse, repeated the command, "Pojo, come," and without looking down, set off walking toward the forest on the clearing's right.

The leash tightened then slackened. A surprisingly easy surrender. Head down, tail held stiffly, he stalked around her and ranged toward the first stand of alligator juniper. His head eased sideways; he was watching, not her, but the canyon.

Still.

He'd given in. But he hadn't given in.

Around the clearing's perimeter she led him, past the junipers, piñon and ponderosa pines, little-leaf walnuts and glorious bigtooth maples, to the rear of the cabin, where the trees thinned out. Only madrones, with their peeling grey bark, clung to the slope above. Pojo sniffed each tree, combed the mountain grass with his nose and sneezed, and glared around like a disgruntled king. Past the little storage shed tucked under the rock face, past the

bathroom vent and window, past the log ends stick-
ing out as they turned the corner. Still not looking
at her. Behind the unfinished barn, as yet innocent
of her equine plans, and past her renovated World
War II Willys MB Jeep, where he didn't even sniff.
Maybe if he knew how much it cost to fill that gas
tank, he'd be more impressed.

When they reached the clearing's far side,
where the dirt-and-gravel road curled over the
mountain's shoulder overlooking the canyon below,
Pojo froze. Again his ears shot forward and he
snuffled, more loudly than the breeze sighing
through the forest branches. One paw touched the
road, then drew back. He sat, staring into the canyon's shadowy depths, nostrils flaring and the tip of
his tail twitching.

As if he could sit there, scenting the wind all
night.

Nope, not gonna happen. The last arch of the
burnt-orange sun peered above McKittrick Ridge,
spying on them, and the warmth was no more than
a fond memory. Shadows lay softly over the clearing,
gathering beneath the branches and slipping silently
across the lawn. Some dried oak firewood from last
year still sat, ready to light, in the firedogs. Tonight
would be a good night to strike autumn's first
match.

"Pojo, come." Without looking — hey, it worked
last time — she turned and headed for the still-open
front door.

Again a tug at the end of the leash, the pressure released a split second later. Yep, she had his
measure. She'd shown him who led their little pack.
The pressure on her neck and shoulders eased.
Buoyancy lifted her steps as they climbed up the
gentle slope. Pojo circled around her, leading the
way toward the cabin. His head still slanted to the

side, keeping one eye pinned to the canyon yawning behind them. Presumably the other eye watched where he was going.

Then again, maybe not. At her little flowerbed, he stepped over the river-smooth rocks that formed the border, rather than onto the worn path to the door. He paused, back arching, and before she caught on, he three-stepped for balance and lifted his leg.

Not on one of the multitude of trees they'd passed in the last hour. But onto her brave, brilliant little yellow and blue pansies.

His head slanted aside. One cool amber eye skewered her. It felt like a sucker punch.

Then he returned to the path and headed for the door.

They hadn't made any progress at all.

2

The fire snapped in the layered granite hearth, filling the big open cabin with enticing wood smoke. On the dining table, the portable radar antenna waited where she'd left it, back panel pushed aside, retaining screws in a canning lid for safety, and ethernet interface card beside the now-cool soldering iron. She'd changed out the chip for something her homemade UNIX system could order around; instead of toting the manufacturer's dedicated control unit along with all her other gear during training, she could now carry just her netbook and lighten her backpack a bit. *At least something went right today.*

Pojo shoved his muzzle past her sheer draperies and peered out the front window, overlooking the lawn and her brutalized flowerbed, then stalked past the gun case and bookcases to the front door, toenails clicking a steady rhythm on the granite tiled floor. After snuffling at the tight weatherstripping, he prowled through the kitchen, across to the loft ladder and rough-hewn support beams, paused at her wooden-frame bed. His back arched.

"Don't you even think it."

That one amber eye slanted back at her, with the cool tilt of his head she was coming to resent. Pojo flopped down on the sheepskin rug in front of the bed with a huff.

She reassembled the radar, tested it with her netbook, then hauled both up the ladder to the loft and stored them with the rest of her electronics gear. The concentrated attention helped her relax, and finally Bonnie laughed at herself. Honestly, the poor dog was probably picking up on her nervousness — she liked dogs but had never owned one before — so it was no wonder he didn't care for her. Well, that was something she could work on.

The yellow sticky note atop the two thick file folders on her countertop claimed the beast ate more than the human population of Culberson County combined, every night. She scooped it out and set it beside the water bowl, at the end of the kitchen counter, then while Pojo scarfed it down, chasing the bowl across the floor with grim determination, she finished off the lasagna leftovers and cleaned up. When he settled again on the sheepskin, she joined him, crossing her legs on the cold floor and ignoring her butt's cringing discomfort.

"See, I'm not so bad, am I? I gave you food."

Again the sideways glance, flickering and cool. If it hadn't been anthropomorphizing him, she'd say contemptuous. The overhead full-spectrum bulbs and the firelight flashed off that amber eye, highlighted his big grey nose, made each cream-and-tan hair in his ruff stand out individually. His coat looked so soft, so inviting. She brushed her fingers through those hairs, stroked his neck and down his back, petted his broad forehead. But he didn't look at her again. His ears didn't fold back in pleasure, and he didn't respond.

"You know what, kid? This could get old real fast."

That monstrous tongue flicked out, over his nose, around his chops, vanished with a smack. His gaze remained fixed.

On the door.

"Is it that time? You wanna do some business before bed?" After all, he'd just eaten. And *that* from a dog this size sure wasn't anything she wanted inside the house. Especially not just before bed.

She scrambled up. When she was halfway to the front door, toenails on granite clicked in a quick trot behind her. Eager panting.

Did she need the leash? Nah, it insulted this independent, intelligent dog. They needed to establish trust between them. And he was so well trained, according to the records she'd glanced through, he'd answer when she called.

Bonnie started to open the door. Pojo slipped out, shoving it aside, and bolted across the lawn.

"POJO! COME, YOU MISCREANT!"

Pounding pawsteps across the hard earth, scrabbling claws on the gravel road. Bottlebrush tail held high, flashing in the last morsel of dusk, then vanishing down the mountain's slope.

And her brand new war dog was gone.

"Well, that was quick." *Frigging, fragging mutt.*

Okay, so she should have grabbed the leash. Too late for hindsight; like him or not, she needed to find the dog. There was a cougar out there twice his size, a coyote pack, javelinas with serious attitude, and if he made it that far, scorpions and rattlesnakes on the Chihuahua Desert floor. Pojo could likely deal with Afghanistan, he'd worked there, but West Texas was a whole 'nother country.

Repeated blasts from the dog whistle, the one that was supposed to bring the brilliantly trained bomb sniffer from the ends of the earth, produced neither hide nor hair. And she couldn't get a signal on the cell phone, despite the military-sort-of-surplus antenna on the roof. Well, signals were problematic at best, here in the mountains and the middle of nowhere. Bonnie shimmied up the ladder to the loft and flicked on the AN/PRC-77 radiotelephone, preset to the park ranger station's channel.

"Pine Springs Station, Pine Springs Station, this is Whiskey Five Zulu." Impatience bit at her. "Neal, Terri, are you there?"

The radio crackled. "Pine Springs Station here, Whiskey Five Zulu. It's Terri, hon. What's wrong?"

"Terri, my new dog arrived today and he's already run off. I'm going to try chasing him down with the Jeep. Leave the channel open for me?"

More crackling as the pause dragged out. Bonnie rolled her lips together. Terri Thomas was sweet and big-hearted; she'd understand hunting for a lost dog, even though the park was closed for the night and the rangers home around a television and fire. But Terri wouldn't approve the hunt without a nod from Neal, her husband and the senior ranger, and while Neal had gone along with Bonnie's plan for a dog and horse, he hadn't hidden his lack of enthusiasm. She didn't like Pojo, at least not yet, but he was her responsibility.

She couldn't abandon him. No matter what Neal said when he took over the mike.

No matter how much, for one desperate second, she wanted to.

"Whiskey Five Zulu," a new, deeper voice said, "this is Pine Springs Station. It's Neal, Bonnie. Go ahead and get your dog. But take a rifle along as well as the radio. I found what was left of another mule deer up on McKittrick Ridge today, a bare mile from the Grotto."

A cold fist squeezed inside her chest. The limestone Grotto was less than a mile from her cabin. If the cougar was ranging that close, then Pojo was in grave danger.

"Copy that, Pine Springs Station. Thanks, Neal."

"I'll keep the channel open for you, hon." Terri's voice again. "Pine Springs Station out."

Meaning Terri would stay up later than she wanted to, until she heard back from Bonnie. She had to find Pojo fast. "Whiskey Five Zulu out."

Radiotelephone and box flashlight on the passenger seat, floodlight in the back, leash and dog whistle in her pocket, and M1 Garand rifle behind the seats with three extra en bloc clips tucked into her belt: ready for the hunt. Bonnie jammed the starter with her thumb and the Willys MB rumbled to life. New tires crackled through gravel, then she eased the Jeep past the alligator juniper and over that steep, blind slope onto the mountain road.

Headlights washed over the forest, swept past tree trunks and somber branches, and finally settled onto gravel as the Willys MB rolled onto the road. The backwash lit the rock face to her left and fell over the slope on her right. Of course, by now Pojo was nowhere in sight. Likely she wouldn't see him if he was; full dark had overtaken the Guadalupe Mountains, the moon hadn't yet risen, and she couldn't make out the top of Frijole Ridge, much less a dog lost in the forest. The open Willys MB wouldn't provide any protection against a hunting cat if it jumped from a ledge above; she was taking an awful chance for a dog she didn't even like, one that hadn't shown any interest in her. Her heart pounded harder. Maybe she should call the adoption people and let them take Pojo back. Maybe that would be the best way to handle this.

But she had to find him first.

At the first switchback Bonnie stood on her brakes and blasted the dog whistle. He'd answer. He had to. Chill night air crept up her arms and worked its way inside her fatigues. Was that a distant bark, buried beneath the rumbling four-cylinder? She set the brake, cut the engine, blew the whistle again, and listened, eyes closing as she strained her ears. The breeze sighed and branches rustled. No, nothing.

The brute could at least have looked at her.

Another try at the second switchback, opposite the Grotto, braking, killing the engine, and blowing the whistle. This time, something rustled to her right and a branch cracked. She scrabbled with the flashlight and swept the beam around as a grey-brown shape ambled downhill and into the forest, not hurrying. Javelina, a wild pig as big as Pojo but with tusks as well as teeth and attitude. No dog.

And no blood. Javelina would eat anything, but the flashlight showed no horrid stains or splashes. She steadied her breathing, flicked off the light, pressed the starter, and drove on.

Another try at the dip, another partway up the climb to the ridge's shoulder, and another atop the saddleback pass, straddling Frijole Ridge's spine. The waning moon rose ahead, a lopsided tear cried by the night. It was getting late; she should return, check in with the ranger station, and let poor Terri get to bed. If Pojo wanted to be found, she'd have found him.

If she was looking in the right direction. If he hadn't left the road at some point. He could have gone deeper into the park, where she'd have to hunt him on foot since she didn't yet have a horse. But if he had followed the road and climbed the ridge, if she was close behind him, the park's border wasn't far beyond. Cattle ranchers shot stray dogs to protect their herds. The bigger and more threatening the dog, the sooner the bullet.

Her knotted innards made mincemeat of the lasagna. What a nightmare. She hadn't seen anything living since the javelina, hadn't heard anything except the Willys MB's engine. No barking, no clicking toenails, no dying animal screams of pain. One more blast on the whistle; one more time listening to the wary night. Nothing. *Sorry, Terri.* Bonnie started the engine and drove on.

She followed the road down the ridge's far side, stopping and blowing the whistle at every landmark. The moon rose overhead; the night slipped past. At the intersection with the lane leading to the park entrance, the locked gate barred her service road, painted metal bars reflecting her headlights. Bonnie slammed her hands down on the steering wheel, slumping in the seat.

Quitting didn't taste very good, but there was nothing more she could do tonight. She owed Terri a call and an apology.

And she owed a lost dog a greater effort in the morning. No matter his possible emotional problems. And no matter her ultimate decision, keep him or send him back. While her decision might boil down to his attitude, finding him didn't.

She backed and filled, reversing on the road, and headed home, miserable enough to spit.

3

Puffing like a steam engine, Bonnie collapsed beneath a scraggly ponderosa pine — *not atop the yucca, the butt wouldn't appreciate it* — with the deepest interior of the Guadalupe Mountains spread like a bowl below her. Atop McKittrick Ridge meant atop the visible world. Rock walls folded and puckered along the ridgeline on either hand, then plummeted in cliffs to gentler slopes far below that rolled into the shadows like mesas. The mountaintop grasses had burned from the summer's drought, leaving shades of tan and brown surrounding her. Only the pines splashed green into the neutral tones.

Morning sunshine peeking over Frijole Ridge and the promise of coffee had convinced her to cut short an irritable and restless night. A hurried scan of Pojo's records while slurping hadn't found any mention of a microchip, which she might have been able to track. She could try radar, of course, but without some method of differentiating the traces, she wouldn't be able to tell the difference between Pojo, the cougar, a mule deer, or a hiker.

Instead, she'd packed the radiotelephone and binoculars along with a quart of water, wrapped the M1's sling across her shoulder, and cut across South McKittrick Canyon to miss the Grotto and any early tourists. No trail in this area; she'd waded through creosote bushes in the canyon's depths, danced across the intermittent stream on stepping stones, and pushed herself, step after grim, steep step, up the opposite rise until she'd met the McKittrick Ridge Trail's lowest switchback. With each foot she'd gained in altitude, she'd cursed Pojo a little worse. By the time she'd scrambled onto the trail, hair plastered to her face and calves screaming for mercy, her language hadn't been fit for human consumption.

Every hundred yards, she'd stopped and blown that stupid whistle. She'd used as much air on that thing as she had for walking. Except for the glorious view, neither had done much good. If Pojo had barked in response, she hadn't heard him.

Was he frightened, out in the wilds without backup? He hadn't seemed the sort of soul to frighten easily. No, he'd seemed — and it bothered her even to consider it — for the few brief hours they'd spent together, he'd seemed like a soldier on assignment. As if he'd had a job to do, something important. And while he'd been glad enough for the expensive dog food, he hadn't let it distract him long from his self-appointed task, whatever that was.

He'd seemed driven. Obsessed. Like some other soldiers returned from the war, not quite right in the head.

And that didn't bode well for any future they might have together.

Pale limestone rocks dotted the tawny soil around her. It trickled from her cupped hand, between her fingers and past her thumb, leaving the pebbles behind. When she rubbed one rock clean on her fatigue pants, shards of something glinted within. Neal sometimes talked about the minerals found in the Guadalupe Mountain's rocks — mica, chalcedony, calcite. A geology field guide might be entertaining.

Maybe more so than the dog.

She flipped the pebble into the void and listened. But she never heard it fall.

"I don't understand you, Pojo." She scooped up another rock, a bigger one, and polished it on her pants leg. No glittery stuff this time, just monotone dove grey. "I don't think I can be what you need. And since all I'm looking for is a dog, not a challenge, not a fight, well, I don't think you'll be all that good for me, either."

This rock she hurled over the edge into space. Her pulse thudded twice, three times, four. A distant click and clatter, soon gone.

"And that's why I think it's best if you go back to the Daisy Hill Puppy Farm, kiddo. Because I already have enough soldiers with weird brains around me. Another one isn't a good idea, especially not one equipped with teeth like yours."

Decision made. But it tasted sour in her heart.

In the backpack beside her, the radio crackled. "Whiskey Five Zulu, Whiskey Five Zulu, this is Pine Springs Mobile. Bonnie, you out there, hon?"

Bonnie tossed aside the pebbles, dusted off her hands, and grabbed the handset. "Pine Springs Mobile, this is Whiskey Five Zulu. I'm on McKittrick Ridge, Terri. What have you got?"

More crackling. "I think we've got your dog."

Like a cave out in the open — that's how she

described the Grotto to anyone who asked. Dripping water had eroded a cupped hollow inside the rock face, deep enough and high enough for a grown man to take shelter, but he'd need to mind his head or rap the calcium carbonate stalactites poking from the roof like massive, dirty-white ogre's fingers. A detour from the main McKittrick Canyon trail led curious hikers to the Grotto, which seemed fitting: most tourists hiked the trail for the canyon's autumn colors and challenging mountain range, not its curious hidden-away geology.

As she approached, a half-dozen hikers slumped at the rock tables and benches, loudly patterned backpacks on the gravel beside them. One slugged from a water bottle, eyeing her balefully as she climbed the rising trail and ducked beneath a maple sapling's glowing orange fringe. Neal stood on the packed dirt and carpet of brown leaves between the picnic area and the narrow path to the Grotto, his six solid feet like a wall blocking the way. His face resembled the limestone rock behind him — pockmarked, forbidding, set in grim, hard lines. He cradled a Mossberg shotgun, broken open, beneath his left arm. Without speaking, he shifted aside and nodded down the path.

To where Pojo stood guard.

The German Shepherd sat stiff and erect in the middle of the path, ears pricked and muzzle low. His coat stuck out in patches, leaf mold and twigs plastered to his hindquarters and back, as if he'd rolled around on the forest floor en route to his sentry point. Those amber eyes, stern and determined, glared at her from the shadows head-on, a make-my-day invitation. At least he wasn't showing any teeth, not yet.

He'd positioned himself a foot before a narrow point in the path, where tumbled rocks edging it on either side and the rock wall's overhang made it impossible to step around him. It seemed odd that a dog had the intellectual capacity to select such a clever tactical position: no one could visit the Grotto without his permission.

"He's not letting anyone past?" The more she thought about it, the odder it seemed. He'd bolted from a comfortable cabin and raced all the way down Frijole Ridge in the dark to guard this spot. Perhaps her first impression of him had been correct. Perhaps the dog was nuts, unhinged by the trauma he'd experienced during the war and not diagnosed by the experts who vetted retiring war dogs for civilian life. Why else would he lay claim to the Grotto, a place she knew he'd never seen before; why was he ready to protect it from all comers? Why not the cabin and clearing, where he'd eaten and found a comfy sheep-skin rug?

Neal hefted the Mossberg, eased a shell from one barrel, then pushed it back in. "You need to move your dog."

"Just shoot the stupid thing." At the stone tables, the hiker who'd glared at her smacked down his water bottle. "Man, we bought a permit for this trail. I want to be on the ridge camping tonight, and if someone doesn't get rid of the brute, I'm gonna sue."

Bonnie bridled. Great; all she needed to make a bizarre situation worse was a big-mouthed hiker with attitude. *Civilian; he's a no-beating zone. Although he could use one.* She shrugged off the backpack and set it aside, then loosened the Garand's sling across her shoulder and left it in place. She could tell already, she might need it. "If anyone shoots him, it's going to be me." *No matter what other, preferable target presents himself.*

Neal finally turned away from the now-flushed

hiker. "That's fine, Bonnie. Do what you need to do."

Pojo still stared at her, at no one else, as if he'd never ignored her a moment in his life. Amber eyes glowed. His expression, stance, mien hadn't changed; perhaps he hadn't blinked during the interlude. Maybe he'd been confused by the similarities between West Texas and Afghanistan. The smells would be different, but the feel of the sand underpaw, the afternoon warmth and overnight chill, might have aroused all the old canine memories of sniffing out explosives only to see his handler cut in half. Had it occurred on a narrow path such as this one? Was he watching her to see if she, too, would dissolve into a patina of red?

Shoot him, as the hiker suggested. Before he could go further round the twist.

And take her with him.

She shook her head, unsure where that last thought had come from. More to the point, shoot him before he could crack and use his impressive teeth for something besides chewing expensive dog food. Clearly there was something off here. Putting him humanely down seemed the logical, prudent thing to do.

Logical, yes. Perhaps. But not *right*. If she simply shot the dog, everyone would be safe and she'd never have to confront those teeth again, but she'd wonder for the rest of her life what she'd missed. The thought twisted her guts. She'd wonder whether she'd given a fellow vet sufficient benefit of the doubt. Whether she'd turned over and dusted off enough limestone rocks to figure out what was going on here, what made him tick.

Whether Pojo was a hopeless case, or whether the one-woman firing squad was undeserved.

Anything else was murder. And the frigging hiker, and Neal, and all the rest of the world could just go hang until she had that answer.

Heart pounding, Bonnie waved at Neal in a "keep back" motion, and stepped onto the Grotto trail.

Pojo stood and shook himself as she slowly approached, a cloud of dust billowing around him and drifting over her on the sighing breeze. She paused, but he didn't seem aggressive. Despite his alert stiffness, he seemed tired, sort of drooping around his edges, as if he'd stayed awake guarding the path all night and the morning, too. And his determination had cost him; a line of reddish-brown pawprints criss-crossed the path, overlapping in spots. He'd cut a pad during his mad scramble down the gravel road the previous evening, but he hadn't let that stop him, either.

Another step, and another. Still no sign of teeth. He held his silence as she held out her hand and when he sniffed her fingers, it was kind of like a handshake between casual acquaintances. Pointedly, deliberately, he sat down in front of her, barring the path and fixing her with an amber-eyed stare.

But no teeth. No savagery. If he'd gone crazy, it was a working dog sort of craziness, trying to do a job that didn't need doing. Not cracking at the pressure and assaulting the hand that fed him.

Her next breath came easier.

"Hey, kiddo, what are you doing here?"

His ears twitched, once at her words and again when she slid her fingers around his muzzle, stroking the side of his head. He accepted the touch without complaint and even nuzzled her hand in passing. But his fixed, intense stare didn't waver. This blue-collar dog wasn't inviting distraction.

Even if his job was insane.

The grey nose, the one that marked him as a

blue Shepherd, scratched against her hand, rough and dry. Didn't that mean a sick dog? It definitely meant a thirsty one. And he'd proven he wasn't going to attack her for no reason. Feeling more confident and moving more quickly, Bonnie retrieved the canteen from her backpack. Before she got the cap unscrewed, he was pushing against her, that fixed stare transferred from her to the liquid promise. She poured water into the cap and he slurped it empty as fast as she filled it.

The canteen would wash. A big dog slapping his muzzle against her fingers like a thirsty Oliver Twist asking for more was unforgettable.

Time to see how serious he was about guarding the path. Bonnie capped the canteen, set it aside — *he won't bite, he won't bite* — then rose to her feet and stepped around him.

Or at least she extended a foot. At the first motion, Pojo ducked ahead of her and froze. Her knee slammed into his ribcage; without even a grunt of protest, he braced his paws and pushed back. His low-slung leverage won the shoving match and Bonnie stumbled sideways into the rock face. Sharp pain spiked in her elbow and she hissed something naughty.

She didn't need to look. "Neal, *don't shoot*. My fault." Whether it really was or not, she didn't know. But she didn't want him rushing in to save her from a nonexistent threat.

The ranger's Mossberg poised halfway to his shoulder. "Are you sure about that?"

Head down, Pojo paced in front of her, quick agitated steps that left a new trail of bloody pawprints across the path. A dead leaf, still golden yellow, stuck to one paw and scraped across the packed dirt, finally falling aside, a red smear across the gold. It blew away.

"No, she's not." The obnoxious hiker pushed aside his water bottle and stalked forward. "Just *shoot* the *dog*."

Without lowering his shotgun, Neal turned. "One more word from any of you and I will escort everyone off park property."

"I've got a *right—*"

Not worth the time. Bonnie turned her back on the drama and brushed off her fatigues. The strong cotton-nylon blend hadn't torn, but the smudge left on her sleeve by the dust-covered rock showed even on the "digicam" pattern's slate grey. She'd be doing laundry tonight, frag it.

What a bizarre thought. Here she was, deciding whether her dog lived or died, and a stain on a shirt designed to hide stains upset her. Or maybe it was the escalating argument back there by the stone tables. A raw edge had crept into Neal's voice and that didn't bode well. He was a calm, patient man, a lot like the rocks he lectured about and loved; if his temper frayed, he'd make the decision for her.

In the middle of the path, Pojo turned. Fixed her with a hard, brazen stare. Grim, determined. As if trying to tell her something.

He sat down.

Again.

In front of her.

Without ever looking away.

The rock-warmed canyon air chilled. A ghost shivered up her spine.

"Everybody stay right where you are."

She'd been blind. Utterly, entirely blind. And she could yet pay for it.

With her life.

4

   She'd learned a little about working dogs during the process of adopting Pojo. One thing she'd
learned: they all had "tells," ways of communicating
a find to their handlers. One common tell, often
used by narcotics dogs at customs stations, was for
the dog to sit.
   As Pojo had been doing.
   Last night up by the roadside, when the breeze
had blown from the Grotto below up to her clearing,
he'd sat and stared down into the canyon's depths.
Twice — once before she'd taken him on a tour of
the boundaries, and then again afterward. And he'd
demonstrated his displeasure when she insisted he
go inside.
   And twice in the last ten minutes, he'd stared
at her, folded himself deliberately, and sat.
   If she was right, it hadn't been the dog who'd
selected this clever, strategic position.
   Bomb sniffer.
   No signal on the cell phone. No way of contact-
ing the adoption people. If she'd read about Pojo's
tell earlier, when slurping coffee and skimming his

records for a microchip frequency, it had vanished from her memory.

She had to trust this obsessed, traumatized soldier. She had to believe him. She could handle being wrong, looking foolish. She couldn't risk the alternative.

"Bonnie, listen—"

She whirled. "Neal, *stay back.*"

Her voice sounded panicked, even to her. The hikers all stood and drew together around the tables, on the side away from her, the deranged woman wearing fatigues and carrying a rifle. Great, just the image of herself she wanted to carry around in her thoughts.

The ranger froze, Mossberg cradled. His eyes fastened onto hers and widened.

"Evacuate the area," she said. "Is there anyone up on McKittrick Ridge?" Hikers weren't supposed to leave the marked trails, but if one did — and she'd done it herself just that morning — then he could approach Pojo, and what Pojo protected, from behind.

Neal shook his head. "No. What—"

"Just get those hikers back to the contact station." She grabbed her backpack and slung it on, ignoring the resuming and redoubling argument back by the tables. She'd need to haul some gear down; she'd need the pack.

Pojo still sat, watching her. A different sort of gleam lit his amber eyes, something happy. When she stroked his head, scratched behind one ear, his eyelids drifted closed and his mouth opened, panting for a few breaths.

"Good dog, Pojo. But you already know that, don't you, smarty britches. Good dog. Now, guard it." His tongue flicked out, licked his nose, and his jaws snapped together. "Guard it."

She ran down the slope, squished through the mud and gravel, leapt over the intermittent stream — *sorry for the bootprints, delicate ecosystem* — and started the long slog up the northwestern slope of Frijole Ridge.

The decision had come to her without thought, but like most instinctive choices, it felt right. Pojo acted as if he'd detected explosives. If she wasn't willing to shoot him in cold blood, then she needed to investigate his claim. She could call Fort Bliss and request an explosive ordnance disposal team ... if she could convince them she wasn't crazy. It might help her case if she could first convince herself of that. Besides, that course would take time and the park would have to remain closed until it was cleared. And hikers travelled from all over the world to see these autumn colors, the most brilliant in the state of Texas. Insisting the park remain closed during its busiest time of the year was perhaps a smaller point, but an element to be considered nonetheless.

The second switchback on her service road loomed overhead, deceptively near. Brown scrubby grass caught at her mountain combat boot. Bonnie staggered and kept climbing, fighting the steepening slope.

Or she could call Theresa, an explosives expert and one of her NATO Rapid Response team members, using the radiotelephone still in her backpack. Theresa, a friend who knew and trusted her, lived only two or three hours away. But the thought of waiting that long tightened around her skin like a prison cell. Not knowing if her guess was right or wrong, if the dog was crazy and she was a fool — no, not a workable solution. She needed an answer soon.

The last ten feet to the switchback rose almost

vertically. She braced her boot against the biggest tuft of grass and pushed up, grabbing a handful more overhead. Sharp thin blades cut into her palm. But she didn't feel blood, no slippery mess making her hand slide off the grass. Pulling from above and pushing from below, she swarmed up the rise, rolled onto the gravel road, scrambled up, and started running.

No, she had only one option — to serve as Pojo's voice and advocate. She had to prove him right and expose any explosives that were planted on the Grotto pathway. Then Neal could call Fort Bliss for a disposal squad and she could let the experts take over.

And if she was wrong, she'd have to shoot the dog she'd only just started to like.

By the time she rounded the last curve and her cabin came into view, the uphill run had settled into her calves, thighs, and lungs. *Wuss, wimp, pansy, pitiful excuse for a soldier.* She sounded like her old drill sergeant; so much for positive self-talk. Ignoring the lead weighing down her legs, she accelerated up the final slope, across the clearing, and body-slammed the cabin's front door to brake.

M9 bayonet from the gun case, hardwood kris dagger from the display above the hearth, portable toolkit and box flashlight from the kitchen cabinet. The two fat file folders still sat where she'd left them on the rustic dining table; no time for them now. She'd decided to trust Pojo, so trust him she would. No metal detector; well, not every bomb contained metal. Up in the loft, crammed full but at least organized, her netbook, a strong tripod, and the radar antenna she'd altered and reassembled only yesterday — the day Pojo had arrived. At least she'd checked her work last night, but now she'd field test it for real.

The tripod's mounting stuck vertically from the backpack's zippered top and the gear sloshed around inside, not filling the space enough to prevent movement. She wrapped bottles of sports drink in hand towels, used rubber bands to secure them, and stuffed the backpack's empty spots, then added a cereal bowl. Pojo could use some electrolytes and after she finished her third hike of the day, they wouldn't hurt her, either. She returned the radiotelephone to the backpack on top of the other gear. Sixty-plus pounds of equipment; she needed to finish building that barn and buy a horse.

At the door she paused. Urgency nipped at her; she yearned to settle this, one way or the other. But if she was right, if Pojo proved trustworthy, she'd be searching for an explosive device in little more than an hour's time. Okay, so her closest friend was an explosives nut, and she'd watched the bomb disposal process, and handed out the tools as operational nurse often enough during training and the war. But she'd never done it alone.

Meaning she might never see her sweet little cabin again.

For a moment the ache was exquisite. But the urgency won. There was nothing she could do about that. Bonnie closed and locked her cabin door, heaved the backpack into the Willys MB, drove to the second switchback above the Grotto, and then backed and filled until she'd tucked it tailgate-first against the rock face; even if the brakes gave way, it couldn't roll downhill. Backpack strapped to her front for now, she jumped from the switchback to the steep slope below and skated down on her butt in a controlled tumble, bouncing over the grass tufts in painful jolts and sending a massive cloud of dust billowing into the afternoon sky.

Guess they'd figure out she was coming.

5

The hikers had vanished. Neal sat in their place, Mossberg on the stone table in front of him, elbow propped, and mountain boots crossed atop the opposite bench. The sun balanced above McKittrick Ridge and the evening's first chill breathed in the lengthening shadows. Not a lot of daylight left.

Pojo hadn't moved. His amber eyes had been fixed on her from the moment she'd ducked under the orange-leafed sapling and the Grotto's area had opened before her. Heard her coming, or smelled her. Or he'd been sitting there watching and waiting. Kind of creepy in a way, and flattering in another. At least he wasn't ignoring her any more.

Bonnie unslung the backpack, crouched in front of Pojo, and unzipped it. He watched her, and if he blinked she didn't notice. Tripod, toolbox, big thick square antenna, netbook, connecting cables — no canine reaction. Still sitting on the pathway, stiff and impatient. Kris dagger; his ears pricked higher. Bayonet, and his tail swished back and forth, scattering leaves across the packed dirt. The universal landmine detection tool. Something he recognized.

Well, whatever made for a happy dog.

"You've got really lousy taste in entertainment, kiddo." She poured him a bowl of sports drink and slugged down a bottle while he lapped — *orange, yuck* — then set both of their empties aside.

"What is all this?" Neal asked. His shadow inched across her shoulder, hesitated, withdrew.

"It's called a man-portable radar." She fired up the netbook and while it booted, she screwed the tripod's mounting bolt into the antenna's base and telescoped the legs to their full length. No need to stretch them open, though; she'd be using it flat and facing down. "It's not exactly the right gear for the job. This is a high resolution radar, working in giga-hertz, and we'd get better results with something in megahertz. But it's all I've got and it should at least give us a clue what we're facing."

"Bonnie girl, what's this job you're talking about?"

The shadows had lengthened across his wea-ther-beaten face, confusing the planes and angles and hiding his expression. His gaze skipped across the jumble of electronic gear. He hadn't figured it out.

Actually, she hadn't told him. But he'd trusted her enough to send the hikers packing and wait on a cold stone bench while she'd run off without a co-herent word.

"The job's ground penetration." *The job.* She'd adopted Pojo's mindset, joined his single-minded de-termination. Or obsession. If he was crazy, he'd taken her with him, just as she'd feared.

And if he wasn't, she had some explosives to find. Great choice.

Neal grunted. "You mean, looking to see what's down there without digging? You really think there's a bomb or booby trap?" He didn't quite laugh. "Way out here in the middle of nowhere?"

So much for trust. She tapped the keyboard, entered her password, and booted up the interface software. "He's a bomb sniffer. Can you think of any other reason he's acting this way?"

Neal's shadow eased away, slipped from off her shoulder, and vanished. "Yeah. I can."

But he still backed up to the pathway's head.

She scooted closer to where Pojo sat, his tail quivering. The antenna was eighteen inches wide, the trail over a yard; so two side-by-side scans would cover it with a third down the middle, overlapping them both, if nothing showed. The tripod would add four feet to her search pattern's reach, letting her explore past the big boulder looming on the right side. As she cleared a section of path, she could inch further forward. At least the dog was no longer pushing her back. But he still stared at her.

The grid faded in on the netbook screen. A quick test prior to starting the search wouldn't hurt. She aimed the antenna back down the path, over her shoulder, and fired off the impulse generator. One second, two, then a greyscale topography of the rocks behind her coalesced on the screen. It was a raw image, not shape-classified, but the human figure standing half behind the biggest boulder, off on the right side of the screen, wasn't hard to spot. Test successful.

"Before you begin whatever it is you're doing, Bonnie, let me borrow your radio. We need to check in with Terri," his voice lowered to a growl, "so that fool woman doesn't come chasing after us and tear us both limb from limb for being idiots."

Hooking one hand around the radiotelephone, she pushed it behind her. "Go for it. But take it back to the tables so I can concentrate, okay?"

Footsteps crunched. His shadow broke over her, switching off the sunlight like a lamp, then it withdrew, the light returned, and the footsteps retreated. "Trust me, I intend to."

She set the antenna face-down on the ground in front of Pojo and tucked the tripod's jutting legs between the rolled-up backpack below and her thigh above. Bracing her boot heel against the dirt and pressing down with her knee lowered the tripod like one end of a see-saw on the backpack's fulcrum, raising the antenna an inch above the ground's surface. Not the most stable arrangement, but it would let her take readings without tripping anything down there. Ready to go.

At the thought, everything inside her tightened. Roly-poly baloney, she didn't want to do this, and the sudden realization thudded in her chest like a panic attack. People died searching out buried bombs and booby traps. Unexploded ordnance maimed and killed people all the time in Vietnam, Cambodia, Korea, Mozambique, Angola, Kosovo, Georgia — Afghanistan, where Pojo's handler had died. Even still in France and Germany, more than six decades after the last war's end. Maybe she should just brush aside that covering of autumn leaves, exposing the path and finding where if anywhere the packed dirt had been disturbed. They didn't blow around with the gentle breeze, didn't even flap; had they been wetted down and glued into a mat to hide a booby trap? Or was she being paranoid?

And maybe her brushing hand would be all the weight needed to trip a bomb's hair-trigger. *Stop, breathe, center.* Beside her, Pojo whined. He still stared at her. He'd finally decided she wasn't useless. Well, maybe he was waiting for additional information; her actions now would help him decide.

She'd been judging him. He'd been judging her. And now it was crunch time for both.

Another deep breath. Bonnie held the tripod in one hand, lifted her thigh, and eased the antenna beyond where Pojo sat, folding herself into a runner's stretch and using one hand to guide the rolled-up backpack. His amber gaze shifted to the antenna, following its motion onto the path behind him, and he whined again. But his tail swished. Behind her, Neal's voice droned, repeating the call-up over and over. This deep in the canyon he'd have trouble establishing contact; she sometimes did from halfway up Frijole Ridge.

When the antenna's closest edge was level with the tip of Pojo's tail, she braced it in position with her leg, its face an inch above the ground. She didn't let herself worry further. Her fingers flowed over the netbook's keyboard, instructing it to start the impulse generator. The ultra-wide band radio waves penetrated the ground, bounced off the irregularities, roots, and rocks within the soil, and seconds later a bizarre, confused jumble appeared on the screen, shades of grey in various intensities reflecting the composition of everything less than a foot below-ground.

There could be a nuclear warhead down there and she'd never see it. She had good penetration, but too many returning signals. Unlike her test with Neal, the raw data were impossible to decipher.

Well, hell. Another problem to solve.

She could scan the entire area, store the data, compile it, and prepare horizontal slices. That would give her a better picture of what was underground at, say, each inch of depth, and she could combine that with the vertical slices to create a three-dimensional image. But she couldn't reach the entire path, not with any degree of safety, and she really didn't want to blow herself up. Especially as any explosion would likely take the Grotto with her. She might survive, but its natural beauty would be shattered.

Not to mention Pojo. He hadn't moved, and watched her research as if he understood her every action. Putting him through another butcher-the-handler sequence would be beyond cruel, if he survived.

Nope, not a good choice. Instead, she could scan and compile the path in chunks, creating those three-dimensional images eighteen inches at a time. That would show whatever was down there, if anything. But it would take all night. Neal's voice, still repeating the call sign behind her, had risen in tone; his patience wouldn't last that long.

So maybe she could filter images by shape. But that would only work if she knew what to look for. With this hardware-software system, it would take time to determine the shape of an underground rock, especially if it was jammed up against other rocks and tree roots. But if she could guess the composition of a bomb, she could instruct the software to search for that particular shape. That would be simpler and quicker.

Worth a try.

Chances were she faced an improvised explosive device, such as a pipe bomb, rather than something manufactured professionally. And some IEDs used explosive materials without a recognizable casing, detonated by a cell phone or remote control. So if she filtered for straight, parallel lines and right angles, or right angles with gentle curves, anything that shape within the chunk of earth she'd just scanned would be highlighted on the screen. She punched in the search parameters and waited while the netbook sorted through the data. Still a jumbled mess. No pipe bomb, no straight lines.

Other IEDs were made from artillery or mortar rounds rigged as booby traps. Almost all such shells had smooth, rounded curves, and those that didn't looked like pipe bombs and would have been winnowed out by the parallel-lines filter. She saved the first set of parameters — she might need it later when searching the next chunk of earth — and entered recognition parameters for bullet shapes. Again the filter came up empty.

"Well?" Neal's voice. She hadn't noticed when he'd quit repeating the call-up.

"Gimme a few minutes, will you?"

"We're losing daylight, Bonnie. There's a cougar out here and I'd rather go home to my wife for dinner instead of becoming his. Not to mention, down here in the canyon, I can't reach her."

The sun hung less than a fingernail's width above McKittrick Ridge. The strong sunlight had vanished while she'd concentrated; the air had chilled and dark fingers stretched from every solid surface.

"There's a flashlight in my pack. You've got a shotgun and I've got a rifle. Pojo will let us know if the cougar's near."

"You sure about that?"

No, she wasn't. He was trained to sniff out explosive materials, not hungry felines. But if he smelled something big and aggressive heading their way, surely such a smart dog would say something. He still hadn't moved, sitting beside her waiting for results. If Neal's patience had limits, Pojo's didn't seem to.

"Just get the flashlight, will you?"

Okay, so not something with parallel lines or right angles, not something smooth and arched. Rounded, like a disk? Couldn't hurt to try. Bonnie saved the bullet-shaped parameters and entered a filter for circles or partial circles. The netbook hummed, the jumble on the screen sharpened, smoothed, and there, at the upper edge, the software highlighted a circular arch as big as a man's palm.

"Oh, hell."

"What?" Gravel scuffled behind her.

"Keep back, Neal. Better yet, get some distance down the trail, say to the hunter line cabin or the Pratt Lodge."

"You're not saying you found something."

The last of the sunlight splashed on his face. Whatever he saw on hers, through the shadows that covered her, it wiped the sneer off of his.

"I think it's a landmine."

Pojo barked, one sharp cracking explosion of sound. Bonnie jumped, her leg's motion rocking the antenna's upper edge perilously close to the ground's surface.

Where the pressure plate would be.

It was the first time she'd heard him bark. Seemed they were finally on speaking terms.

Right when it might be too late.

6

Dusk blanketed the path. Bonnie rested one hand beside Pojo's hindquarters — his weight was sufficient to trigger a landmine, so she knew that ground was safe — leaned over the path, and carefully brushed away the leaves and thin upper level of dirt. A depressed circle emerged, less than five inches across, its leaf green plastic dirty but obvious against the pale grey-white of the path. In the plastic's center, soft black rubber in a smaller circle sported four stubby, flat legs in an X-shape across the mine's upper plate. The rubber pressure plate rested a millimeter below the surface.

Landmines were almost always found in herds. She stretched out further, to each side, leaning against Pojo's unmoving, sturdy bulk for balance, and brushed more leaves aside. Another one. And another. At least four of them, arranged in a dia-mond pattern in the trail's center and only a step beyond the little red-pawed path Pojo had paced. He'd protected all of them.

And she'd nearly shot him.

No wonder her dad had told her to never have

kids. *Stupid people shouldn't breed.*

Neal's voice hammered away again in the background, this time with real urgency. He hadn't gone far, not nearly as far as she'd ordered, but of course it was his park and she really shouldn't be ordering him around at all. Suddenly the monotonous crackle of static was broken. Terri replied. No honeyed Southern tone now, but shrill words, intense in the gathering night and interspersed with loud staticky bursts. Whatever was wrong was really wrong. Bonnie shook her head and shook it off. She'd hear about it later.

With the wooden kris dagger, she dug beneath the first mine and levered it from the path. The green plastic circle was about two inches deep and weighed maybe a pound: a Soviet-era PMN-2, one of the worst, most destructive anti-personnel mines ever made. It contained enough Composition B explosive, similar to the bang stuff within World War II artillery shells, to blow off a soldier's leg. Not a comforting thought, considering how close she held it to her body.

When the USSR collapsed, more than one weapons stockpile had simply vanished. Someone, some hopeful indiscriminate murderer or terrorist, had found one on the black market. She snorted. *Probably an auction website.*

She couldn't afford to lose her temper or her nerve. It had been a year since she'd practiced clearing minefields. But she'd hung out with Theresa, her friend the explosives expert, long enough for the basics to remain clear in her mind. She had to pry out the fuse without triggering the little button in the center of that black rubber X. And to do that, she had to take the mine apart.

Risking setting it off.

She had to do this. The dog sitting beside her

didn't.

"Pojo, go."

He looked at her, eyes glittering in the deepening twilight. He'd seen his previous handler cut in half; he knew what explosives were, what they could do. Smart as he'd shown himself to be, she'd expected to see him frightened, or if he hadn't made the causal connection, wearing a normal blank doggy expression.

He astonished her.

He looked happy.

Pojo finally moved. With a yawn, he lay down beside her and began licking his cut front paw, a steady slurping in the forest's hush.

Stupid stubborn idiotic frigging fragging mutt. "Pojo, GO."

Slurp. Slurp. Slurp. A blatant case of determined disobedience, kind of like a sit-in. He might as well carry a picket sign reading *Civil rights for working dogs.*

But she couldn't misunderstand his message. Pojo had seen one handler cut in half. He'd rather risk it himself than see another one go the same way and be left alone again.

And as a fellow vet, she had to respect that.

Deep breath. Calm.

Carefully keeping her palm arched away from the pressure plate, Bonnie flipped the landmine over in her left hand. Two socket screws were inset into the bottom plate, in the nine o'clock and noon positions. The largest Allen wrench in her collection fit well enough, although it wasn't the proper tool for the job. Hard turning pressure, one good jerk, and she tumbled the first socket screw to the path. A startlingly bright hot pink flashed beneath it, orange beneath the second one. First step successfully done.

Slurp. Slurp. Slurp. Steady, comforting. A calming rhythm for her dance with their deaths.

The hardwood kris wasn't sharp enough to saw through the rubber surrounding the pressure plate, but the edge on her bayonet opened each leg of the X by a good inch and she ripped the black stuff off in shredded pieces. A copper disc in the X's center, hinged to the plastic, fell aside and exposed the tiny steel nubbin of the trigger. *Don't touch it. Don't think about it.* The pressure plate itself, also copper and in the same X-shape as the rubber, was held in place with little plastic strips. She pried each aside without letting the plate push against the trigger, and it fell off into her hand, trigger and all.

The worst was over. And they were still alive, she and Pojo. Slurp. Slurp.

And then his head came up. His lips lifted, showing those huge gleaming teeth, pale in the night. A bass rumbling spilled from his open jaws, echoed from the Grotto's cave, shot through her like straight chilled vodka. He'd changed his mind about dying with her. Now, when the trigger was naked in her hand.

"Hang on there, Bonnie." Neal's voice. Tense but not afraid.

The flashlight beam swept past her, down the slope and into the stand of young maples surrounding the Grotto's clearing, past where she worked. Buried within their low-hanging cover, something big moved. Something really big. The light stopped, steadied, and two huge eyes, level and unblinking, glittered in the beam. Pojo's snarling rose an octave.

"I'm gonna fire. Don't jump."

Good thing Neal hadn't gone far. "Sounds like a plan."

The Mossberg cracked like a metallic whip.

Behind her, but not over her shoulder; aiming off to the side. The eyes blinked, vanished. The motion behind the saplings stilled. Of course Neal wouldn't kill the cougar, only drive it away. She sucked in air; at some point she'd quit breathing and her throat ached as if she'd been throttled.

Pojo hadn't flinched at the shot. Hands shaking, she set the green plastic in her lap and stroked his big head. Soft fur under her palm, gritty with dust. "Good dog. Good soldier dog."

The rumbling snarl eased. He stared off into the night. Then he twisted his head, slurped that sloppy tongue across her trouser leg, and returned to washing his front paw.

"I want you to know that was disgusting." But at least it hadn't been across her face.

"You okay, Bonnie?"

"I'm good. One more minute here, okay?"

The kris dagger had been a gift from her commanding officer and was not something she wanted to lose. But bayonets were cheap. The steel point bent at the pressure, but it levered up the mine's bottom plastic plate and she ripped the two halves apart. The spring from the pressure plate tumbled aside, and there beneath it was the fuse, looking like an innocent square-headed bolt. The yellow half-ring of Composite B, molded around the center components, gleamed briefly in the flashlight's beam.

She tugged out the bolt, and it was done.

"So that's what a landmine looks like." Neal squatted beside her. "Little bitty thing, ain't it?"

"Told you to keep back."

"Not good at following orders. Which is why I'm the ranger boss."

"Yeah, as much as Terri lets you." Bonnie opened the last bottle of sports drink, poured half into the bowl for Pojo, and drained the rest. "What was she upset about earlier? It sounded nasty."

Neal shot her a glance, quick and unhappy, then he twisted aside and slumped on the rock by the path. "Seems they weren't lucky enough to have a bomb sniffing dog at Carlsbad Caverns or on the logging trails up in the Lincoln National Forest. A hiker died before they could get him to the hospital and a park ranger lost a leg." His voice dropped to a mumble. "A man I know." He sat still, as if lost in thought, then he leaned over and ruffled Pojo's ears. The Shepherd didn't glance up. Slurp. Slurp. "Stubborn brute. So what do we do now?"

"If you'll hold the flashlight, I'll take care of these other three mines." Better not mention she hadn't done this since the war. If he didn't want to be scared away, she wouldn't try harder. That cougar was still out there. "Then we'll get back to the contact station and you can call Fort Bliss for an EOD team. You'll have to close the park until they're done demining the place."

"Terri's already called them and a team's on the way. Homeland Security's saying we've got a home-grown terrorist cell attacking national parks, so we'll close until they sort it out and make some arrests." His hand moved toward Pojo's head again. Amber eyes glowed in the darkness, one swift glance, and Neal scratched his own face instead. "And you? What will you do?"

Surely he knew that without asking. She huffed. "I gotta take care of my dog."

★ ★ ★ ★

She wanted to carry him back down the trail and save his poor cut paw. But she desisted at the deep rumble in his chest. Instead, Bonnie tugged off her socks and fashioned booties for him, cutting the soft material with the battered bayonet, doubling it over for thickness, and tying them around his lower legs. Pojo sniffed at them, gave her that narrow amber-eyed look she'd come to appreciate, but tolerated them as an acceptable compromise.

They plodded down the trail to the contact station together. Neal would drive them to the Willys MB, parked on her service road, and she'd drive them home.

Whenever they paused on the trail, Pojo leaned against her and washed her trouser leg. Slurp. Slurp. Slurp.

The soldier dog had come home.

- 30 -

AFTERWORD

Like most of my favorite stories, *Shakedown* is a blend of fact and fiction. Guadalupe Mountains National Park, McKittrick Canyon, Frijole Ridge, and the Grotto are all real places, rising from the rugged Chihuahua Desert and butting up against the Texas-New Mexico border south of Carlsbad Caverns. The canyon contains a magnificent riparian forest along an intermittent stream, and hikers, both well-behaved and otherwise, come from all over the world to see the autumn colors. Of course, you can't really live in a national park, but that's the story's fictional part. And I can dream.

As well, you really can adopt retiring war dogs from Lackland Air Force Base in San Antonio, Texas, home of the adoption program. About three hundred of these magnificent animals find homes every year. First consideration is given to the dog's handler, second to police departments that have need of a working dog, and third to the general public. Most of these canine heroes are over ten years old and have health issues. While there's no charge for the adoption, civilians are expected to pay for the dog's transport home. For more information, see:

http://www.jbsa.af.mil/news/story.asp?id=123279 665

http://www.37trw.af.mil/shared/media/document/ AFD-120611-035.pdf

Roughly four thousand people were killed by old minefields in 2010 and about ten thousand injured or maimed. Every year, forgotten landmines resurface. Volunteer organizations around the world are working to clear these leftover war zones in Africa, Asia, Eastern Europe, and South America. One such organization, the HALO Trust, offers more information at this website:

http://www.halotrust.org/

ABOUT THE AUTHOR

Hi, I'm Gunnar Grey. I write books. I'm a historian, political junkie, target shooter, and retired adventurer and equestrian. I read avidly and post reviews or at least ratings for most of the books I read. Occasionally my poor husband surfaces from beneath a pile of paperbacks, gasping for air... but I shouldn't bore you with personal issues.

I live in Humble, Texas, just north of Houston, with four parakeets, the aforementioned husband (who's even more entertaining than the birds), an orange betta fish with no manners, a fig tree, the lawn from the bad place, three armloads of potted plants, and a coffee maker that's likely the most important item we own.

blog: http://the1940mysterywriter.weebly.com/blog

website: http://the1940mysterywriter.weebly.com/

Twitter: @JGunnarGrey

Also by J. Gunnar Grey

starring the NATO Rapid
Response Team

Star of Wonder

Christmas Eve, noon

"*No*, I don't want off the team."

The Christmas tree lights reflected from Captain Kenneth Rutland's USMA class ring, the matte gold flaring red, then green, then back to red in boring, predictable monotony. The least the decorator could have done was plug a random flasher in line with the light set and stir some lovely chaos into the mix. Unless, of course, the decorator had *wanted* to lull everyone to sleep. Maybe, but unlikely, since the lights were turned on in the middle of the day. Non-engineers just had no imagination.

And the living room around them looked like the same decorator had sprayed out holly and ivy and mistletoe and pine branches with a firehose. Little red berries; little red balls. Tradition was good; tradition held the culture together. Tradition could be overdone. Big time.

Didn't help that the decorator in question was his boss' sister.

"Not only no, but hell, no. You can't get rid of me that easily." Kennie drummed on the coffee table, in time to the lights' flashing rhythm but throwing in a few flourishes of his own. Somebody needed to liven the place up. "I'm just asking. I went to school to learn how to build things, not destroy them." Not that there was anything wrong with that, as the conservative snark went.

Colonel Robert "Sherlock" Holmes, in civvies topped with a sweater, peered down at the laptop balanced on his knees, his eyes scrunched into slits. The scar on his forehead stretched where it disappeared into his hairline. Gingerly, he tapped a couple keys, pausing between taps. Then he stopped and refocused on the screen. Kennie wanted to scream, just from watching that pitiful performance. How could anybody move so slowly with a keyboard at his fingertips? He could do better with a pair of pencils. Or spatulas.

And as he'd done for the last hour, Sherlock ignored him. So much for sitting down for a serious conversation. The downside of visiting his commanding officer over the holidays: putting up with his typing. His sister's decorating. His teenagers' boisterous noise. And his supercilious I-don't-want-to-deal-with-it attitude. The upside—

Well. He'd have to think about that one.

"Why don't we ever go to another country and put something together for them? Why are we always ripping their stuff apart?"

With a frown, Sherlock slid reading glasses from his pocket, deliberately unfolded them, and arranged them on his face. He shifted focus long enough to glare over the frames at Kennie's drumming — *okay, okay* — then turned back to his work. "You mean, besides the irreparable damage it would cause Theresa and her pyromania? We sometimes do build stuff, ya know. Maybe you're forgetting our drilling project—"

"Nope." That slow Texas drawl took forever to reach a point, even when there was a chance one might be in the offing; Kennie had quit waiting for Sherlock to finish his sentences long ago. "Water wells are good. Everybody needs to drill a well once in his life. Still not what I went to school for."

Tap a key. Flash red, flash green, flash red. Tap another. Seriously, the trip to Houston was starting to look like a massive mistake, even worse than Washington's latest regulatory boondoggle. All he'd wanted to do was spend some private time, away from the generals and the rest of the team, convincing Sherlock to expand their job description; NATO, their overseers, gladly provided civil support to its member nations, as well as military intelligence and combat operations.

"Our average, median, generic job is to sneak into a third-world nation, steal an uninsured truck from some poor schmuck who can't afford the loss, drive halfway across nowhere on roads the average highway department would declare a total loss, pass communities that need far more than a few organizers, ignore a couple hundred vital building projects where a little help would go a long way — so's we can release a few political prisoners from jail. And blow up the place behind them."

Another glare at his hands; somewhere during

that tirade, he'd started drumming again. Kennie leaned back and grabbed the recliner's arms, digging his fingers into the smokey blue leather. If he held on hard enough, maybe he wouldn't start drumming on the laptop's keyboard. Or his boss' head.

"And you know, and I know, and everybody else knows, after we leave the bad guys are just going to send their secret state *polizei* out on another midnight sweep. In a few months, they'll have just as many political prisoners as before, only now they'll be in somebody's drafty old warehouse or stinking cold basement. One of our team will be sporting a new ache, we'll have more blood on our hands — in the long run, what difference does any of it make? Buildings last. Dams. Roads. Even sprinkler systems. But reform-minded individuals in banana republics have a limited catch-and-release shelf life."

Tap. Flash green. Now the lights reflected from Sherlock's glasses, the shiny lenses and metallic frames, and from the subdued red scar encircling his wrist as he poised one finger over the keyboard. Kennie waited until the finger began its descent.

"A guy should have more to celebrate on Christmas Eve. That's all I'm saying."

Sherlock muttered something ugly under his breath and reached for the backspace key. "Why don't you go out and get some exercise, 'stead of staying cooped up in here, peering over my shoulder while I'm trying to get some work done?"

Like he wasn't fighting fit or something. "...exercise?"

"Always a good place to start." Sherlock's voice trailed off as he tilted his head back and stared at the screen. Sharp brown eyes sharpened further, peering through the bottoms of the lenses.

Oh, lovely. His commanding officer, the man who led them in the field, needed bifocals to see his computer screen. That wasn't anything to celebrate, either. "Right. Well, clearly I could be spending my time in worse ways." Kennie eyed Sherlock; *for example, talking with you.*

Sherlock eyed him right back; *you sure could.*

Kennie sighed. "Don't y'all have some big sort of park nearby?"

"Sorta, yeah." One eyebrow canted. "Why, you looking for a lift?"

Like hell. Kennie stalked to the door, grabbing his iPhone and punching up the map app. The comical plastic case mocked him; it looked like an engineering nerd's pocket protector, yellow mechanical pencils and red and blue fountain pens perfectly aligned above its built-in amp and speakers. Cute and bright and not where his career seemed to be headed. "No, I'm not looking for a lift." He'd rented a car at the airport. Under his breath, he added, "Not from a blind man."

"Think I didn't hear that?"

If his commanding officer's ear quality matched his eye quality— "Whatever."

"Heard that, too. You are carrying, aren't you?"

Kennie paused, one hand on the polished brass doorknob, frustration reaching for a seismographic spike. He didn't need a mother hen, and the SIG Sauer P225, in a crossdraw above-the-belt strut holster, hidden beneath his untucked polo shirt, symbolized his dilemma and never let him forget it. "Of course. Aren't we always?"

No answer. Again.

Kennie refused to slam the door behind him.

* * * *

Memorial Park. Of course. Wasn't there a

Memorial Park in every city in the nation? the world? Surely they'd blown up a couple of those, too, sacrificing playgrounds, soccer pitches, golf courses as diversions. Not that golf courses mattered; stupidest game ever invented, even stupider than watching liberal talking heads on cable. At least this Memorial Park had an enhanced jogging path, an exertrail; he could break the monotony of straight-and-level forward motion with some strength-building.

Not that that sounded appealing, either. Exercise. Sheesh. What had he done to deserve that brush-off? Besides piss off his commanding officer, of course.

A handkerchief-sized lawn bordered the jogging trail at the park's entrance. Kennie sprawled on the dry, withered grass and started stretching.

The trailhead lay at the intersection of a busy street, Memorial Drive, and an almost empty one, Memorial Loop. Heavy traffic piled up behind the signal lights, mere yards away, spewing lovely noxious chemicals into his lungs. The crushed-granite jogging track curved in a boringly predictable arc, following the block's inner perimeter. Oodles of joggers and a few bikers thronged the track; lots more chemicals where those came from, and lots more lungs with which to share. Red bows festooned the streetlights, signal pylons, and most of the pickup trucks idling at the light; one SUV the approximate size of a medieval cottage sported wire-and-felt reindeer antlers.

In the park proper, pine trees and oaks towered over dense underbrush, as if shielding something primeval from the common view. Kennie snorted and flexed into the stretch, breathing in the musty blend of earth and grass, the ground's cooler temperature seeping through his cotton sweatpants.

Even at winter's start, on Christmas Eve, some of the trees held onto their leaves, and the still-green underbrush was sufficiently thick to discourage anyone from wandering off the governmentally prescribed path. Beneath the musty earth and chemical exhaust lingered the crisp, Christmasy scent of pine sap.

Texas. Fabulous regulatory climate. Produced more jobs than the other forty-nine states combined. A great place to live. Until you ran headfirst into the heat and humidity. Then you'd be lucky to make it out from behind the Great Wall of Texas alive.

Frustration welled up in his chest. He'd spoken nothing but the truth: he didn't want off the team, even if he was sick of their average, median, generic job. Honestly, if one more political prisoner called him a hero through the bars of a cell that was about to be blown open — well, there were more personal locations where Theresa could plant her explosives. Problem was, she'd think it a great idea.

Maybe they were heroes, he and the NATO team. If so, the title was overrated, kind of like the Nobel Peace Prize. Possessing said title sure wasn't enough for real Christmas Eve satisfaction, no more than Sherlock's bifocals. And unfortunately, it seemed Kennie's attempt at broadening their job description wasn't going to get far.

Damn it. Maybe an impassioned plea to his boss' boss at their January training camp? And when had he, Kennie, become so cynical? Hard to say what had caused it, his job or Washington. Most likely some devilish combination of both; with the donkeys in charge, you'd think their assignments would have migrated more to the positive end of engineering. Instead...

Deep in a runner's stretch and lost in thought,

Kennie spied movement behind him, back in that thick underbrush where no movement should be. He held the stretch and focused through the stream of passing joggers.

Afternoon sunlight filtered through the pines' high canopy and spilled across the treeline's edge, highlighting the underbrush of dark green yaupon and forming a demarcation point between the jogging trail and woods. Above those bushes peered a horse's head. A dark bay the color of good rich loam, darker on the face, and a wisp of black forelock drifted between its ears with the gentle breeze. Bold gleaming eyes watched the joggers, skimmed over the traffic, and glanced up at the red ribbons blowing on the streetlight above Kennie's head. Its deliberate attention swept past Kennie, moved beyond him, then paused and doubled back.

The horse's gaze meshed with his, staring back across the yards of grass between them. Then a passing jogger broke the moment. Kennie started. But the horse didn't look away, and again he found their mutual stare intensifying. The next jogger was merely a flash of motion, unimportant and ignored.

Besides the intensity of its stare, something about the horse seemed odd and out of place. But Kennie couldn't put his finger on what bothered him. Horses weren't that unusual in big cities, of course; he'd seen romantic horse-drawn carriages hauling tourists and lovebirds through downtown Houston, and his map app had showed the polo grounds and stables were near Memorial Park's amenities. But there weren't riding trails through this section of the park, and besides—

A ripple of curiosity rolled through him. The horse wasn't wearing any tack. No leather straps encircled its head, neither halter nor bridle. And no rider sat on its back. Nobody stood near it. Nobody ran around screaming, "Loose horse!" For that matter...

Kennie ripped his stare away — strange, how much effort it took — and glanced about. Nobody looked at the horse. Among the steady stream of joggers pounding the track, ten feet from the horse and treeline, nobody even seemed to notice it. Two curvy blondes power-walked past, their arms pumping five-pound bar bells, their tongues wagging as jogging traffic piled up behind them. A tall, slender man with an expensive haircut pranced almost in place rather than run on the grass, waiting impatiently for an opening in the steady stream, then he lowered his chin and ducked around the blondes.

None of the exercisers even glanced aside to where the horse's big head protruded from the underbrush, in clear view.

He looked again. The horse was gone. But *something* moved among the trees, something big, writhing and twisting back where the shadows exerted their camouflage. The motion stilled, then the shadows parted and a woman stepped into the horse's spot.

Not just a woman. A beautiful woman. And she stared at Kennie with her eyebrows drawn together and her chin tilted, as if trying to figure him out.

Although tall enough to see over the bushes, she squeezed past them into the sunlight. Dark hair cascaded in gentle waves to her shoulders, strands swaying in the same breeze that had teased the horse's forelock. A brown linen shirt molded to her upper body, black cargo pants to her legs. Black boots, not quite combat boots but strongly built for hiking or outdoor work, completed an impression of sturdy capability sans fashion; whatever she set her mind to do, she'd likely achieve it. With one hand she pushed the last branch aside, paused in the light without squinting, then approached him, a slow smile tugging at her lips.

Kennie scrambled up, his pulse starting to pound. Lithe as a cat, she stepped behind a mountain biker, slid between two congregations of joggers, weaving a graceful path toward him without ever glancing away. Weirder yet, not even the guys turned to stare at her. Tall as she was, fit and sexy, moving like a panther through the dedicated exercise fiends — she wasn't a woman to be ignored.

The warming fire in his blood proved that. He wasn't a sucker for a pretty face, but he knew he could happily stare at her for a long, long time. When he hung out with the team, gorgeous women looked at him last; even Sherlock's savage scarring scored higher than his strung-tight-as-a-mad-cat tension. And yet this woman never glanced away from him, and her lips curved into a promising smile.

Texas was looking up.

* * * *

*A psychological mystery from the
acclaimed author of Deal with the Devil*

TROPHIES

J. GUNNAR
GREY

Trophies

current time

Three neat entry wounds drilled through the silk of Aunt Edith's blouse, stiffened and blackened by crusted blood. The underlying color was unrecognizable. I only knew it was supposed to be green because she wore it during our unfriendly dinner the previous evening and I remembered. Lying on the sidewalk with her legs crumpled beneath her, she seemed even tinier than normal, like a toy that had been roughly played with and then pitched aside.

I dropped to my knees beside her. Her eyes were wide, staring at the dawn breaking beyond the storefronts, and her mouth gaped. She was such a private person, so contained, elegant, brilliant as gold beside the base metals of the rest of us. Death seemed an exposure, a stripping of her secrets. A humiliation.

I reached out to stroke the drifting black and silver tendrils of her hair into place. But a hand snatched my wrist and twisted it aside. I jerked my head up—

—the picture window of the Carr Gallery, just overhead, was splattered with something dark. More of it sprayed the polished maple door, the brass railing and handle and mail slot. A small hole in the door, at waist level, had been marked with chalk—

—more dark stains, lit obliquely by the dawn light, trickled down the red brick, dripped from one concrete step to the next, painted the sidewalk. I suddenly realized I could smell it—

—I ignored the background *crump* of artillery fire and panned the rifle's scope along the enemy emplacement, atop the ridge overlooking our sand-bagged trench. Beneath the camouflage netting and wilting tree branches I made out one big field gun with its muzzle recoiling, another, a third—

—the enemy spotter stood contemptuously in full view, binoculars to his eyes, gazing off to my left but sweeping this way. The rangefinder showed the distance at eight hundred meters. I set the elevation turret and aligned the sight's upper chevron on his center of mass, drifting aside by one hash mark to compensate for the gentle flow of air across my right cheek. Binocular lenses flashed sunsparks. His lips moved as I took up the initial pressure on the trigger—

—flashback with visual, auditory, tactile, and olfactory hallucinations. Hadn't happened in months. It was impossible to prevent it, stop it, tone it down, or predict its arrival. But we were intimate enemies, my flashback and I, and I knew its script. I clenched every muscle I possessed, including my eyes, and froze in place, ignoring it all. It's how I'd taught myself to respond when the city street morphed into a battlefield without warning, and so far it had prevented anyone from locking me up. I was even able to fool most acquaintances into thinking I was still sane.

But nothing blocked the sights, sounds, or other manifestations. Machine gun fire hammered into the nonexistent sandbags, thuds echoing in my bones, and the dust and acrid gunpowder caught at the back of my throat. Someone screamed, a long shrill sound that climbed higher in pitch and volume, scraping across my nerves. The enemy guns chattered again and a fire of agony spurted across my back. Wavery, sick-feeling blackness rushed in behind the pain. I refused to wobble. I ignored the war zone and the adrenaline tearing me apart, and waited for the screaming in my damaged memory to stop. For several more seconds it dragged on, a horrible rising shriek, but finally it cut out in its usual abrupt manner, as if someone hit a neurological mute button.

The flashback lost. It couldn't control my actions nor force me to betray my internal damage to the civilians. I wanted to collapse with relief. I refused to do that, too.

Ambient city noises resumed. There were lots of voices around, both live ones and the scratchy overlay of radio transmissions, and in the distance someone called my name. Even with my eyes squeezed tight, popping emergency lights strobed across my retinas. I still smelled the blood.

I failed Aunt Edith. Everything inside me wrenched. I failed her and now she's dead. That particular fear, of failing someone important, always followed the flashback. Knowing it was coming never prevented the reaction. I wouldn't show that, either.

Only when I knew I was back in real time did I open my eyes.

Dawn and Boston had returned. The battlefield was gone, replaced by the street of upscale shops, converted from historic red-brick row houses. Picture windows with discreet painted logos and black wrought-iron bars alternated with concrete steps rising to entries, each landing decorated with trees or flowers in wooden barrels. Blood painted the steps and façade of the Carr Gallery, Aunt Edith lay dead and hidden beside the entryway stairs, and there on her other side was a doughy face like something a baker played with before rolling it out. Its expression was outraged and the hand attached to the equally doughy body still gripped my wrist, our arms crossing above Aunt Edith's neck.

"Don't muck up my crime scene, man," he said in pure Brooklynese.

Ice clogged my veins. My field of vision constricted until all I could see was his face before me. I could control my physical behavior during the flashback and even my awareness, once I realized its game was on; I couldn't chain the emotions, nor the adrenaline. The muscles I'd released tautened again. Flight wasn't an option, but pounding something was. "She's not a crime scene."

He glanced down, as if only then realizing Aunt Edith was, or had been, human. "She is now."

I went for him. But strong arms hauled me back and away.

One of the live voices sniggered in my ear. "What a circus."

No sense fighting. It wasn't the policemen restraining me nor the crime scene technician I wanted to pound. I wanted the spotter, the one that got away during the war. If I could find the murderer who'd dossed down my Aunt Edith, he'd do, as well.

"Charles!"

That was my cousin Patricia's voice, piercing the enshrouding mental fog. I ignored the hands gripping me and peered over my shoulder. She stood alone, makeup smeared and lipstick chewed off, in the midst of the curious bystanders behind a strip of yellow tape. Flimsy as it looked, that tape represented the boundaries of the permissible and therefore was sufficient to stop her. Had they put that up behind me? I couldn't remember seeing it, much less ducking beneath it.

Patty seemed safe, so I turned back to Aunt Edith and eased from the policemen's holds. But a man stepped between the crime scene technician and me — between Aunt Edith and me. "Mr. Ellandun?"

I looked around him and didn't bother being subtle about it. Aunt Edith stared back, the heavy emptiness of the dead replacing her usual honest and level gaze, neither judgmental nor compassionate, with something blank. One of her pumps had fallen off and a chalk circle had been drawn around it. A bit of trash; the most amazing woman I'd ever met, and she'd been tossed aside like a bit of trash. It was beyond wrong. It was obscene.

"It's captain, actually," I said. "Captain Charles Ellandun."

He kept speaking, but as usual, Aunt Edith dominated the scene without trying. Only now it wasn't her elegant vivacity accomplishing that feat, but its absence. She had been the Rock of Gibraltar in my life since I'd been eleven and meeting her had been the watershed moment of my watershed year.

She'd always been vital, compelling, more alive than the city itself. It was impossible for her to be dead.

Her skirt was the same as last night, as well, woven wool in the Hunter tartan plaid, the one she'd worn the day I first met her. Likely she'd returned to the art gallery directly after dinner, then. She still wore her wedding ring, as usual her only jewelry. There was no sign of her purse.

"Captain?" It was the man who'd stepped between us, a plainclothes detective in a button-down shirt and dark slacks.

Pounding him wouldn't help, either. I forced myself to look at him. I even remembered his question, although I was too distracted to focus. "Yes, I own several handguns."

"And were you in the war?" His voice was professional, beautifully modulated, and easy to listen to, even at that moment.

Even if he was an irritant.

"Yes." Was I ever.

The long, drawn-out *skrip* of a closing zipper demolished all my good intentions. The doughy crime scene technician slowly sealed the body bag. The shadow of the canvas flaps fluttered across her blank eyes. Then she vanished inside.

The air left my lungs as if I no longer needed oxygen, either. Again tunnel vision narrowed my field of focus, this time to the gurney as it rumbled past. The technician's hand rested atop the lumpy canvas.

I yearned to go for him again and fought the flashback-induced impulse. Although the battlefield had vanished into the scattered recesses of my mind, the subconscious, primal scream of combat still goaded me. Then I caught up with what the irritant standing beside me had just said in his elegant tenor.

Where were you last night.

I stared at him while the implications of that question soaked into the corners of my damaged brain. How long that took, while we locked eyes and assessed each other, I don't know; accurately measuring time has never been one of my finer accomplishments. But the details of his perfect face — expensively styled bronze-toned hair rippling above his ears, brown eyes steady and suspicious, smooth tan that had nothing to do with working outside, not a trace of stubble on the square jaw — left an afterimage on my retinas like the strobing emergency lights. How could he stand being so damned perfect? It didn't matter whether pounding him would help or not. I went for him instead.

Again hands hauled me back. And suddenly cousin Patricia was between us, grabbing handfuls of my sport shirt and shaking me, or at least it. "Charles, for God's sake, what is *wrong* with you?"

I nearly told her, nearly reminded her of my diagnosis, but couldn't see the point even if I was an Ellandun and lived for the fight. The gurney and the moment were gone and the bloody adrenaline finally snapped. I shuddered beneath her clenched fists as the aftereffects kicked in. From the way her already wide green eyes were stretching wider, she felt it, too.

"Charles?" This time, her voice was less than a whisper and it broke in the middle of my name.

If I could have stopped the shaking, to protect Patty I would have done it. I'd failed her, too, and again I closed my eyes. Whatever showed in my all-too-transparent face, she didn't need to see it.

Because I'd tried to tackle a plainclothes police detective, Boston's finest slung me into the back of a squad car to cool down, one of an armload of emergency vehicles scattered about the street. They closed the doors, too, and how the July heat that rapidly built up inside that car was supposed to help me cool down, I cannot imagine. The interior stank from the stale fast-food wrappers littering the floorboards and the stain of something I didn't want to identify on the part of the seat I avoided.

I'd put up with all of it if I could have Aunt Edith back. She couldn't possibly be dead.

Outside the patrol car and a few yards away, Patricia and Brother Perfect chatted like old friends, her eyes sliding sideways to check on me every minute or so, his never leaving her damp and smudged face. He'd positioned her so she couldn't see the blood. Her mousy brown hair strained back in a knot that looked painted on, but then so did her jeans, and with her streamlined figure, I'm certain the average male never noticed the hair. To give him credit, Brother Perfect's gaze didn't drop, not even to her green cotton camp shirt, halfway unbuttoned from the bottom and tied in a knot above her belt buckle. Perhaps the stained handkerchief she used to rearrange the sad remnants of her makeup put him off.

Finally she walked away, ducked beneath the yellow crime-scene tape, and waited outside the perimeter, staring at me in the back of the squad car with her lower lip between her teeth. Brother Perfect watched her until their eyes met for a brief glance, and then he turned, opened the squad car door, and slid into the front passenger seat.

To give him further credit, he didn't bother scolding me. "You say you have several guns. Tell me about them."

I rubbed my eyes. "I own an M-16, a Mauser sniper's rifle—"

"Handguns, Captain. Tell me about your handguns."

To hell with him. I moved over until I breathed the outside air. "I have a Colt .45, two old Walther nine millimeters and two new ones—"

"What's the smallest bore handgun you own?"

The question threw me until I realized the holes in Aunt Edith's lungs had been small. "The nine millimeters."

"No twenty-two?" he asked. "Nothing smaller than a nine?"

"No," I said.

He stared at me for a long moment. The shakes had diminished as the adrenaline ebbed away, leaving me taut and intensely aware, and the skeptical curl of his lip made his opinion of my veracity perfectly clear. Again my temper began heating — there was something about him that made that a delightful process — but I swore this time I'd hang onto my self-control.

"I've kept records," I said. "And my LTC Class A and FID are both in order. You're welcome to check them."

"Thank you." The tone of his voice left no doubt he'd do so whether I volunteered them or not. "Are you carrying now?"

"No." But I intended to rectify that as soon as possible.

"So where were you last night?"

"At home." I gave him the address of my condo on the waterfront, north of Burroughs Wharf and well away from the tourist congestion at the Aquarium and Rowe's Wharf. He didn't write anything down; perhaps he had a photographic memory. "I had dinner with Aunt Edith around seven, got home around nine thirty or a bit after, and stayed in."

She had tried to persuade me to be sociable and forgiving, get involved with her latest bloody art show, see the family while everyone was in town as if I had a particle of interest whatsoever in them. The remembrance of how little encouragement I had given her during that, our final conversation, set my insides squirming.

"Can anyone confirm that?"

I hadn't even checked email. "No."

That internal squirming had a distinctly frigid tinge to it now. He'd gun for motive next; wasn't that how they did it on those stupid cop shows?

But he surprised me by motioning me out of the car. He leaned atop the hood, his perfect face strobed by the popping emergency lights so that he seemed dipped in blood then wiped clean, over and over again. I knew that image would stay in my nightmares for a long time to come. Something else to appreciate about the man.

"Don't leave town," he said, and walked away.

* * * *

Thanks for reading! Dingbat Publishing strives to bring you quality entertainment that doesn't take itself too seriously. I mean honestly, with a name like that, our books have to be good or we're going to be laughed at. Or maybe both.

If you enjoyed this book, the best thing you can do is buy a million more copies and give them to all your friends... erm, leave a review on the readers' website of your preference. All authors love feedback and we take reviews from readers like you seriously.

Oh, and c'mon over to our website:
            www.DingbatPublishing.Weebly.com

Who knows what other books you'll find there?

Cheers,

Gunnar Grey,
publisher, author, and Chief Dingbat

δ
Dingbat Publishing

www.ingramcontent.com/pod-product-compliance
Lightning Source LLC
Chambersburg PA
CBHW070646130626
46555CB00006B/2731